In Search of Amika

MultiMind

First paperback edition, Sept 2020
First e-book edition, Sept 2020
First audiobook edition, Sept 2021

Library of Congress Control Number: 2021914535

Cover design by Ejiwa Ebenebe

ISBN 978-1-952860-00-3 (paperback)
ISBN 978-1-952860-01-0 (ebook)
ISBN 978-1-952860-02-7 (audiobook)

www.multimindpublishing.com

In Search of Amika

$\mathcal{A}$nother night, another night. Keyona was quite tuckered out from her day. She would have loved to have been tired from back-to-back meetings and water cooler chats but instead, it was more "Sorry, another qualified candidate was selected" replies. Three popped up on her phone that day, one via text, the rest through email. Her job-only inbox was cluttered with either "Thank you for applying" or "Thank you for your application but..." emails. The only things that broke up the monotony were the spam letters she received from the countless mass recruiters she signed up with. She used to trim her inbox but now, she hardly saw any point. Apply here, apply there, remain unemployed no matter where.

Her days were monotone, just like today. Do more resume work, search countless job boards, apply to whatever or wherever barely matched her skill set as a computer science kid with a fresh degree and four years of university debt. *Go into comp sci,* they said. *You'll always have a job,* they said. Keyona knew her case wasn't unique; every other kid that didn't want to be a doctor or a lawyer was told the same thing. And now, they were all in the same boat: young, educated and desperately looking.

She had a few little blessings here and there but rarely did they feel that way. Keyona had an apartment with no roommates but it was small, cramp and crowded. She could fry eggs from her bed, walk three paces to the right and stumble out of her "cozy" abode into the drab apartment complex hallway. Paid for by her parents back home in Atlanta, they wanted to make sure no worries distracted her from her studies as a second-generation graduate. It would be a dream, if it were a good thing. Instead, they would check on her constantly: to see how she was doing, see if she had any food in the fridge, see if she was working yet. They figured Delaware had more to provide than Georgia for tech degrees and jobs while far less expensive than New York or Silicon Valley, California. If they couldn't physically swing by, they would call. Every time, her parents, Marissa and Terrance, filled her with encouraging words but they were always salted with the pressure to find *something*.

Keyona knew what would happen if she didn't find something fast, they would let go of the purse-strings and tell her to figure it out herself. Their patience was already worn thin by buying the college apartment in the first place four years ago. They never wasted an opportunity, either. Up until she was a junior, they reminded her here and there that when they were her age, their parents *never* paid their way for anything, it was *expected* to be out and independent by eighteen.

Beyond the miserable pick-up jobs Keyona had applied for countless times already, the land of employment still laid a bare wasteland. She applied to a couple more and looked out her tape-sealed window. Dull stars and a half-lit moon hung well in the sky. It was time for bed.

Too depressed to shower, Keyona changed into her sleep clothes, an over-sized gray shirt she won during trivia night back in college and a long satin cloth wrapped over her lengthy braids. She was lucky to get her hair done in the past week, a braider needed her laptop fixed and Keyona needed a long-term style. She may or may not have dinked around a bit to make the problem appear more complex than it actually was but it got her the beautiful waist-length microbraids she wanted. It was the closest thing she had to a good job since she graduated. Her satin wrap tied up secure, Keyona climbed into her creaky, twin sized bed. It was stiff and flat, and held the same mattress she had since middle school, but it was still a bed. The coral sheets were comparatively newer, a house warming present from home. Her moon pillow stood out, lumpy and possibly in need of a wash but still soft and comforting. It was the first thing she bought when she moved in, along with the fuzzy star-covered blanket it came with. She drew the blanket up close and hoped for a restful sleep.

❧

Deep in the middle of the night, the sheets became like quicksand. Curled up and slumbering, Keyona began to sink into her bed. Her blanket slowly deflated under her disappearing silhouette. Her head slid from her pillow.

When her foot kicked brisk space and air, Keyona stirred. When she tried to push away, to get her foot back on the bed, it went nowhere. She jostled awake. Blurred by shock, and blurry tongued by sleep, Keyona yelped fuzzy words for help. She clutched her blanket for grip to sit up but the shift of her weight just made her sink faster. Then, she was gone.

The air shredded past her as the starless night sky slowly turned to dawn. A low sun graced the horizon but the second sun underneath it gave the streaks of mountains and plains a burning glow. Keyona tumbled wildly down, tangled up in her blanket. The drilling rattle of its corners filled Keyona ears. She could hardly make sense of anything, let alone see anything clear enough. The world wouldn't stop swirling about her until she stopped struggling to unfurl the

blanket from around her. What she did see terrified her –
land. Far, distant land that grew far less distant by the
second. Bewildered and clueless, she tried to unfurl the
blanket again. She thought it would make for a suitable
parachute but soon stopped, she couldn't come up with any
positive examples of that working outside of cartoons. Her
heart sank deep into her stomach.

The land was wide and rustic, webs of villas and cities
sprawled out between the lush forests. Rippling mountains
were everywhere, stark and with long shadows over a third
of the land. The calm ocean glittered with gentle waves.
What a lovely sight Keyona would have adored, if she wasn't
plummeting to her certain death. One minute, she was
sound asleep, dreamless and snoring. Now, she was soon to
be splattered upon strange plains and meadows.

Or at least she would have, until she dropped into a cyan
blue sandpit. All that poked out was a corner tuft of her
blanket and nothing else. The soft grit of the sand wasn't
invasive; she could breathe but she still kept her blanket
clamped shut over her nose and mouth, her eyes winched
shut. Outside, there was a voice, a single voice but
cacophonous. It chimed and clattered over a helium pitch,
fussing and babbling.

Dread rattled through Keyona as her mind raced, *Am I
dead? Did I die in my sleep? I'm dead, aren't I? I am dead. I died*

in my sleep and I am dead. This just happened. I died from misery in my sleep. She took a deep breath and sighed. *Wait. Do dead people breathe in the afterlife?*

Around her, the sand shifted and moved until it lifted her up to the surface. Flecks of sand were stuck against the dark brown of her skin, a couple bits tumbled away. The blanket had bits of flecks as it draped down her front. Keyona kept her face buried, afraid of what she would see.

It was cool and quiet, still and pleasant. She wasn't falling anymore but she wasn't sure she was somewhere better. Sounds carried light echoes; she was indoors. And around her shuffled about an anxious, odd ... someone.

"I didn't think! I didn't think! I thought you could fly! Or that you'd land here! Where are your orbs? Why didn't you hover?" The jingle in their tone rang like strangled bells. They were beyond flustered. "Amika, what were you *doing* being aimless in the sky? I thought you knew where I was?" The voice paused and the shuffling stopped. "Amika?"

Keyona felt a small poke in her fleshy side. She tensed up and tried to scoot away on the sand but only sifted it about instead. She remained silent.

The voice asked again, a slower drawl but the jingle just as tight, "Amika?" After another soft poke, they apologized with a looser jingle, "I didn't mean to make you fall. You've been missing for a while and I've been trying to find you since Rulo became ridden with hunters–"

"Who is 'Amika'?!" Keyona demanded, her face sprung upright. Her deep Southern accent was irritated and annoyed. "My name is *Keyona*. Who are y– Why am– WHAT IS HAPPENING?! *Am I dead*?! I'm dead, ain't I?" She stared helpless and lost at the figure before her. They had medium brown skin, double pointed ears and a sharp, angular face. Their eyes were as light as snow, only a faded line marked out their irises. Their lashes and brows were the same, light and soft as snow. Their hair was thin strands of clear blue glass beads folded into a neat, long braid. They wore puffy, grey pantaloons and a stitched plum tunic banded at the waist with several ropes and satchels. Their face wore a befuddled, silent stare.

"You're not Amika," the stranger's voice jangled low. "Who are you?" Above, the light orbs illuminating the moss-covered cottage home brightened a little more.

"Not 'Amika'!" Keyona lanced. Her anger slipped into desperate sorrow as she spoke, "I'm *not*! My name is *Keyona*! Look, if I'm not dead, please send me *home*. I 'on't mean *no* harm, I just wanna get *home*–"

"I made a mistake," the stranger mumbled to themselves as Keyona continued on. "How? I did everything right. Who is this strange person? Why–" The stranger talked louder over Keyona's pleading, "Why do you have Amika's spirit scribe? How did you get–"

"What 'spirit scribe'?" Keyona clapped her legs on the sand, annoyed once more. "What are you talkin' about? I ain't got no 'spirit scribe'! I just graduated university a few months ago–"

"Wait, you're a Scholar but don't have *any* scribes?" The stranger was even more confused than before.

"No! I got a degree from Delaware University but that's it! Can I go *home*, please? *Please?*" Keyona wanted to cry but she wasn't sure if that would help or harm her situation. The stranger looked odd, and their home was even odder, a stone cottage covered in spates of moss. Bottles and jars with unusual writing lined the walls in neat rows. Colorful, spindling plants floated next to closed wooden windows. A couple hovered low over a table or two across the cobblestone floor. A weathered, leather tome laid on the ground next to the pit, pages sprawled. Floating candles and glowing spheres lit the space close to the thatched, dome ceiling. She decided to hold it in.

The stranger approached slow and cautious. There was little they could believe the unusual person before them was saying. With a serious jingle in their deepening tone, they asked, "How do you have Amika's spirit scribe–"

"*I 'on't know!*" Keyona blustered. "What it look like? I *swear* I ain't got it! All I got on is a sleep shirt and this here blanket! No pockets!" Keyona sorted herself atop the sand best she could for maximum modesty and flapped out her blanket. A slight plume of sand fluttered from the blanket's snap. "See? Nothin'! Look, ma'am – or sir! – I'm just tryin' to get *home*. I'm real sorry that I'm not who you thought I was but I never met Amika and–"

"You have her *scribe*. It's in you!" The stranger accused. Their lashes and eyes drifted from snow to a faint violet. Keyona fell silent upon the change. The stranger's voice rang a deeper chime, akin to a grandfather's clock, "I did *everything* right. *Everything*. That ring Amika wore was *not* easy to find after those people took her house and *torched* her belongings. Either you're *lying* and took it or you're *her* somehow. And I knew her well, so *talk*." The light spheres above the pit began to dim and descend. Keyona hugged her blanket tighter. "I will forgive *no* lies –"

"Wait, WAIT! I'm not lyin'! What does it look like?!" Chill fled through Keyona's veins. For a fleeting moment, she thought falling would be better.

"A sea blue gem with writing in it." The stranger stood at the rim of the pit, anger and disdain painted all over their face. They stuck out a slender hand and looked down their wide nose at Keyona, "Give it to me. Now."

Keyona was at a loss for words. All she had was the truth. Or what she thought was the truth. She tried to eke out the words that broke through her fearful silence, "I … I don't have … it? I never …never seen anything like that in my life. I'm from 'Lanta. Please … *please* don't hurt me, I ain't – I ain't a thief. Never stole nothin' in my *life*. I'll – I'll help you find Amika somehow, can … can that work?"

The stranger looked over Keyona with a suspicious gaze but their eyes and lashes returned to snow and the spheres lifted again. With a silent incantation from the stranger, Keyona rose from the pit with a delicate float and was placed on the ground. Rattled, Keyona clutched her blanket. Standing there, her quivering legs gave out and she collapsed onto her rear.

"You *still* have Amika's spirit scribe. I can sense it," the figure explained, their voice ascending to a medium jingle and a dull tone. "*You're* going to be my compass. Once we find Amika, she will explain everything. Then, you can go home. I spent too much of my soul and my time to happen upon a mistake now. Get up and let's go."

Keyona pulled herself to her feet. Her legs still shook, she willed them to not give out again. Whoever this person was, she didn't want to cross them further. Blanket drawn close to her chin, she softly quaked, "Can I … can I ask a question?"

"Go ahead," the stranger obliged, bemused.

"Am I dead?"

Silence engulfed the cottage. Keyona's eyes were wide and still, affixed on the stranger and their flat stare.

The stranger broke out into fitful laughter. "You better not be!" Their voice carried a light tinkle in their pitch, like a shaken bell. "The ritual wouldn't have worked, otherwise."

"Huh?" Keyona asked through the stranger's laughter, "Then where am I? And who are you?"

Winding down, the stranger answered, "You're in Rulo, on the Northern seas of Hesult. I'm Ipkuni. This is *definitely* not the Otherlands. Amika is my close friend and I'm determined to find her."

The day stretched on far longer than Keyona had ever experienced. With two suns, there were two of everything: two mornings, two noons, two evenings, all two hours apart. Given only a pair of russet fur slippers for her feet, Keyona spent her day walking about, through the dense forests and dusty backroads of Rulo, clueless and tired. Ipkuni trailed behind in their sturdy gray boots and a plum cape with a smooth gait, skeptical.

Keyona tried to adapt the best she could to traveling. Her satin covered braids were twisted into a low bun. She tried to fashion the blanket into a wrapped skirt to cover her legs but it dragged on the ground. She tried doubling the blanket up, but it became too hot. Instead, Keyona sighed from embarrassment and tied the blanket around her neck like a cape. It kept her cool with the breeze it caught and gave her proper coverage, and she didn't have to fear bending over. Ipkuni couldn't care less what Keyona did or how she fared. They just wanted to find Amika.

As they walked along a tenuous grassy path beside a rushing river within a dense forest filled with bulbous trees thicker than any redwood back home, Keyona made her way over a rocky, sliding patch, "Hey, why – and don' fling me into the river or anything but why is it so hard for you to find this 'Amika'?" she asked. "I mean, if y'all were close–" she stumbled on a hidden rock and almost choked herself stepping back on her cape.

Ipkuni rolled their eyes and cursed the stars for receiving such a bumbling idiot. Deep in the forest, they figured the both of them were safe enough to speak freely, and if not, that the idiot would serve well either as decoy or bait to get away and try the ritual again.

With a petulant sigh, Ipkuni explained, "She is in deep hiding from the hunters. Far and wide, they have come to collect her for her scribe. They usually expend their energies chasing down troublesome vagrants and slippery bounties on the run from the law but they ... Amika is seen as a bounty. She's done no wrong and never has but her scribe ... makes them see different. Amika has a Scholar scribe but it never looked normal. They're supposed to be the color of sand or parchment – the color of innovation and intelligence – but hers was the color of the sea. A beautiful scribe. She had always been a Scholar, but so much more than that also – she could fly, she could float. She could create illusions as intricate as the world around us. There's not a trade or craft she couldn't master. Not simply know it but *master* it. Very un-Scholarly. So that made her beyond exceptional ... and a threat."

Traversing a terrible, rocky incline with fluid ease as Keyona tried not to topple over gracelessly, Ipkuni continued, "Hunters want Amika because they think she has special abilities that can aid in their more ... 'pressing' aspirations. Such as wiping out odd spirit scribes or making them secretly work for the hunters while in bondage."

Keyona eventually fell behind, bedraggled by a burdensome rock that she became winded on. Her slippers provided no comfort from the terrain, every stone and pebble could be felt underfoot. Daggers jabbed her calves from the soles of her feet in every step. She wanted nothing more than to stop. She hobbled behind Ipkuni.

Unconcerned as they passed Keyona, Ipkuni kept on, "Amika could see the boom falling but I simply didn't believe her. I was the one who convinced her to stay, that she was overly fretful. I ... I just didn't believe her. And she narrowly didn't escape because of me. No goodbyes, no nothing, just... nothing." Ipkuni slowed, haunted by their choice. Their failure to believe and protect the one person that mattered the world to them. "I saw them torch her house," they trailed off. Ipkuni picked up the pace again, "It's – it's what woke me up. It was the middle of the night and there were loud crashing noises. I thought a miller's shed had fallen but everything was much too bright for the nighttime. I got up and simply saw all these ... people – these people just drag out her belongings: her books, her bed, her clothes, her *everything*, and set them alight in front of the house. I never felt so helpless. I thought she was in there, I was just too scared to rush down to make sure she wasn't. I ... I didn't want them to get me, too. Then, I heard everyone talking about how she wasn't there and that she fled while they burned her things." Ipkuni stopped, which gave Keyona opportunity to catch up. "I simply just *have* to find her. To make this up to her and to get rid of the hunters. They've been in Northern Rulo every day, refusing to leave until they find her. They don't know all that she's capable of, just that she's either useful or better off dead."

Out of breath and struggling to close ground, Keyona huffed, "Why ... why they ... why they not gonna leave? ....

She ... she can fly .... Could be – oh shi– anywhere by now," Keyona had slipped on a rock she thought was stable but shifted underneath. Ipkuni stopped and turned to watch her, bemused again. Breathless, she continued, "An' you ... you wanna have her ... get rid of the hunters?"

Ipkuni's eyes and lashes turned a quick topaz in surprise. "No! Of course not. My stars, I would never do that. I just want to hide her and make a diversion that would get the hunters to leave. They're hateful, not smart. They see a dead scribe, they tend to go away. Amika makes brilliant illusions. I'm not as good as her at that. I can keep it up for a little but she can keep it up for what seems like forever."

Keyona finally caught up with Ipkuni and dropped to the ground. The weather was cool and breezy, the air smelled sweet. It was much better than the Atlanta heat and the Delaware cold but never in her life had she ever travelled so much by foot before. And never would she ever want to again.

"Tired already?" Ipkuni doled out blithely, "It's only half past second noon. You take a lot of breaks for someone with a spirit scribe stuck in them somewhere."

Waving dismissively, Keyona sliced back, "Yeaaaaah, it must be buried *real* deep somewhere because I *certainly* can't feel it. Otherwise, I'd be flyin' *everywhere*. Where *are* we goin', anyway? And why can't you fly or somethin'?"

Astonished, Ipkuni narrowed their eyes and cocked an eyebrow. "For *Amika,* my dear *compass. You're* the one who has been walking us out and about all of Rulo and through even some of the hills of southern Bordavia. The least you can do is withstand your own trails. Amika can fly, I can only float myself or others and only at half-height of a bipki tree, at that. Flying isn't ... normal around here." Ipkuni looked away, they didn't want to make Amika seem as unusual as she truly was.

Keyona rolled her eyes. She had enough of being "compass". Even back home, she was useless *with* a GPS, why ever would anyone ever use her as one *now*? She pointed a flat hand, "Look, I *don't* know where she is. Ain't got the slightest clue. Don' know what to feel for or sense, nothin'. Why, she could be back in my world." Ipkuni was stricken as Keyona continued blindly, "I mean, I nev' been here and if I got the 'spirit scribe' or whatever, she prob'bly in our world – my world, I mean. Like, think on that, okay?"

Ipkuni stared agape at Keyona. That was it, perhaps. The idiot finally proved useful.

Their voice took on a light muted jingle, "She might not actually be here .... She might be where *you* came from!" Ipkuni hurried past Keyona, back the way they came, "Compass, we must go back to my home, we *have* to find–"

"*All* the way back?!" Keyona called out behind them. "Are you *serious*?"

Ipkuni charged forth, "That's where all my books are! Come, compass!"

Keyona dropped her head. "Even *more* walking, fantastic," she muttered.

The duo returned to Ipkuni's home, the small stone cottage was burrowed among a small stretch of houses in sparse and rustic villa. Life in the villa was robust. Animals dallied about or trailed owners, and the center square down the road bustled with busy markets and loud merchants. To the left of Ipkuni's home was a brick and sunstone house. The windows were bashed in, the door gone from its broken hinges. Dark and trashed, sunlight filtered through the rubble. In front of the house, a blackened pile of refuse. Nothing could be made out from the pile – not a chair, not a photograph, not a bed. This was Amika's home.

In Ipkuni's house, Keyona and Ipkuni sat together in the cyan sandpit. Ipkuni read from their tome as it floated before them, mouthing countless incantations as they scrawled jagged script and jaunty sigils into the sand between Keyona and them. Bound in tired leather and faded calligraphy, Keyona tried to make out the scribble script but understood none of it. Anxiety buzzed restless within her as she sat wrapped up in her blanket. She was glad to return to her world but did that mean she was going *home*? She didn't know this Amika person, probably never met an Amika in her life – at least, she never came close enough to have their "spirit scribe", whatever that was. She only suggested Amika being in her world as an excuse to have Ipkuni take her back.

"Ipkuni?" Keyona asked, cautious. She didn't want to disturb any important incantation or concentration.

Steadily focused, Ipkuni acknowledged her with a flat voice and medium jingle, "Keyona?"

"Will this work?" Keyona pulled her blanket tight, specks of sand flittered down.

"It should." Ipkuni drew odd, interlaced circles next to the sigils between the two travelers.

"Are you almost done?" Keyona glanced at the floating candles and light spheres around them. They were bright and still.

Before Ipkuni could reply, they dropped through the sand. The lights went out and the tome tumbled off the lip of the pit.

The ground was cold and flat, different from Ipkuni's bumpy cobblestone floor. Keyona and Ipkuni stirred painfully beside each other. The world around them was chilly, dark and silent.

Ipkuni squeaked out, "Do the stars forsake us or are we now in your world?... Compass? Keyona?"

Keyona croaked, "I 'on't know. Did we just literally drop into a dark pit? Where are we?" She had been dumped onto her rear, pain cascaded throughout her spine and hips. Her blanket sprawled about her, Ipkuni kicked off the bit covering their foot. "Did you make another mistake?" she groaned.

Ipkuni felt jabs like salted daggers in their shoulder and side. They winced as they tried to move, their voice creaked like dull bells, "I never made a mistake. And I did everything perfectly this time, I know it. You are the compass," Ipkuni tried to prop up with their better shoulder, grunting, "and should know where you are. And where is Amika. We had better be close."

Keyona tried to gather her blanket to soothe her throbbing pain but it provided little comfort. "I can't see anything so I can't tell. Light this place up and I'll figure it out."

Irritation started to overlay Ipkuni's pain. They hissed a vexed sigh and laid back down to trace a circular sigil on the ground. Spheres of light bled from the floor around them. They bathed the space in a dim glow.

There were bookcases everywhere stuffed with journals, binders and stacks of loose papers. All over the marble tiled floor, dusty cardboard boxes were stacked atop each other, sagged by time. Some sat on top of clear or colorful storage bins.

Looking about, it dawned on Keyona that she recognized everything. "We're in the storage den? Why am I at my parents' house? Ipkuni, we're back in 'Lanta."

"'Lanta'?" Ipkuni echoed. No matter what they looked at, everything looked so stark and foreign. "Where is that? Can you sense Amika anywhere?" Impatient, Ipkuni drafted themselves up from the ground into a stationary float. They drew in a deep breath and clanged, "AMIKAAAAA." Their voice rang like harsh metal bells under their medium bass tone.

Overcome with panic, Keyona sprang to her feet. She tried to pull Ipkuni back to the ground, "Shuduuuup!" She hissed pulling on their tunic, "My *parents* are here!"

"AMIKAAAAAAA!" Ipkuni blared louder. They looked around and spotted a white door behind Keyona. The brass knob cast a shadow twice its length. Ipkuni raised a hand to it, the door clapped open and they started to leave. Keyona struggled to pull them back in but her body ached too much, she soon had to let go. Propped against whatever was near, a box, a door, a wall, she followed Ipkuni into the hallway.

Ipkuni shot a cold glare over their shoulder, their eyes and lashes a firm violet, as they demanded, "Compass, guide me." The hallway was long and narrow with tan carpet and velvet red walls. Flower portraits lined the hall.

Keyona couldn't help but be bewildered and dumbfounded as she stared back at them, propped against the wall. A spike of braids jutted out over her shoulder like a waterfall. "Are – are you *serious?*" she sputtered, "Amika can't *possibly* be here. *I* live here."

Ipkuni's glare grew more intense. Their eyes and lashes became a deeper violet. "Compass, you *dare* deceive me?" They turned around and drifted to her with an ominous toll in their voice and the violet shifting darker, "Either *you* know where Amika is or I suppose I must pluck with my own two hands–"

"Keke? What you doin' here?" a Southern, mature voice spoke from behind Keyona.

Startled, Keyona whisked around. It was her mother, Marissa. A light summer dress adorned her round figure. She was a head taller than Keyona and three times as wide. On her confused face, she had dimpled cheeks and gray eyes. Her wavy hair bounced around her shoulders; she still kept her hair flat whereas Keyona never learned to perm.

Marissa asked, "Baby, what is goin' on–"

"Amika! You - you *aged!*" Ipkuni's eyes and lashes lightened up to a soft blue. They zipped pass Keyona to get a better look at Marissa, who looked just as baffled as her daughter appeared horrified.

"Ipkuni, 'dat's my *momma!*" Keyona blurted out. She couldn't have been more mortified. Dressed in a sleep shirt, furred slippers, a blanket cape, and a satin cloth wrapped into a bun with a strange floating person confusing her mother for some lost soul, this was all too much. She turned to her mother, "Ma, he thinks you're somebody they lookin' for -"

"Amika, where have you *been?*" Ipkuni inquired over Keyona. "My stars, I've looked for you for many suns! How did you get here-"

"*Ipkuni!*" Keyona pled, her mother still mystified between the both of them. "Please shut up! Her name is *Marissa!* She's from Charlotte, North Carolina! Not. *Amika.*"

"She *is* Amika, Keyona!" Ipkuni fussed back. "I'd recognize her anywhere. My dear Amika," Ipkuni clutched Marissa in the tightest hug. Marissa was still lost.

Keyona tried to pry them apart, "Momma, he's just really missin' somebody. Ipkuni, stop! Ma, he just confused! Ipkuni, get off!"

Unfazed from Keyona's feeble pulling, Ipkuni looked over their dear friend, Amika. "Why did you give some of your spirit scribe away? It was so hard to find you! I wound up locating *her* instead," they nodded at Keyona, who still kept pulling, "and she had most of it! I sense you barely have any left! Did a hunter find you in this world? They've subsided some in Rulo–"

"Ipkuni!" Keyona wanted to restrain from shouting in front of her mother but a bit more volume popped out of her than expected. She could hardly hold in her fury and embarrassment. "Ma! Ignore him, please! He's really confused–"

"I'm not! Keyona, stop pulling!" Ipkuni tried to shrug off Keyona's frantic yanking. "Leave me, compass! I am *done* with you!"

"Both of you!" Marissa snapped. She had enough of the commotion.

Ipkuni floated back in surprise. Keyona shrank away. Both were silent. Marissa glared at Keyona and then Ipkuni. She lingered on Ipkuni longest. Ipkuni lowered to the floor with hopeful bated breath, their eyes and lashes faded pallid and snowy.

Marissa couldn't figure it out but eventually something clicked. "Ipkuni?" Keyona almost started up again, Marissa silenced her with a raised finger. "I think I remember you."

In the storage room, the trio talked. And talked. And *talked*. Lights on and door shut, nothing disturbed their chatter. Not even the loud, clumpy return of Keyona's father, Terrance, when he came home from another taxing day at work. He simply plopped down on the living room couch where he turned on some football and eventually fell asleep. No matter how much they talked, Keyona was still perplexed by it all.

Sitting on a storage bin, Keyona rubbed her eyes languidly. Marissa sat beside her on a sturdy box, lively as ever and chatting away with Ipkuni, who floated cross-legged before the both of them. Keyona's blanket was draped across her lap, her bun let down and her satin cloth fixed. She still stretched her shoulders to assuage the dull throbs in her back and hips. Listening to Ipkuni regale her mother with an old gathering story, she had enough.

"Ok, ok, ok," she broke in, quieting her chuckling mother and Ipkuni. "There is *so much* I don't understand."

Still snickering from the story, Marissa asked, "What's wrong, baby?"

"Everything!" Keyona exploded. "Ma, why you ain't tell me that you from another planet or somethin'? Liiiiike, does Dad know when y'all got married or somethin' or naw? Like, I don't understand *anything*. How come I never seen you fly or nothin'? I just – I just don't *get it*. Why you ain't never tell Ipkuni where you was at the whole time? I mean, y'all just need to break it down to me again. I 'on't understand why all this is happenin'. I thought you were from Charlotte, not from deep space!" Keyona was beyond frustrated. How much of her mother's life was a lie? How much of *her* life is a lie?

The smile faded from Marissa's face. She rubbed her hands in thought and glanced at Ipkuni. So caught up with reuniting with her dear lost friend after decades of hiding, she forgot how lost Keyona would feel about everything, no matter how many times she explained. Ipkuni stared daggers at Keyona.

"I'm not from deep space," Marissa replied. "I'm from another world." She reached over and gave her daughter a consoling squeeze on the knee, "I know all this must seem so weird, Keke. I practically forgot my old life myself. I ran away when I was so young. I was frightened and people were looking for me, bad people. I just couldn't turn back, I had to start anew where they couldn't find me but I didn't know where. I simply landed in Charlotte and tried to live as secretly as I could in fear of more suspicion. Mascara and contacts for my eyes, wigs for my hair, illusion scribe for my ears. It's how I met your father, baby. He helped me change my name and everything. Eventually, we fell in love and moved–”

“So – so is *he* just like y'all?” Keyona blustered. Even the *umpteenth* time around, none of this made sense to her.

Taken aback, Marissa replied, “No! No, not at all. Your father is a normal man, honey. He just met me when he was in college. He saw that I was lost and homeless and gave me his old housemate's room until I got myself together. He just thought that I was from a different country and escaping a bad home. I didn't even have a Southern accent, I picked it up from being here a while and to better hide myself. Keke, I know this is all hard to believe but I didn't want to impact your future with my past. Especially since you inherited some of my scribe when you were born. I still float sometimes, just when the house is empty so I can remember the old times.”

Still flustered, Keyona stumbled out, “So, what you – what you sayin' is ... *you're* from a different world on the hideout and just decided to start a new *life* here and ain't tell nobody? Does Dad know that you got all this goin' on? And why can't I fly or nothin'? Did you know that I would or not?”

“Honey, your father would never understand,” Marissa softly explained. “And I don't want him to. He's fine with lovin' me as Marissa, Amika is just too much for him. If a hunter crossed his path, he wouldn't know it and neither would the hunter. And that's the safest for the family. I didn't know that Ipkuni was still lookin' for me all this time." She flashed a kind smile to Ipkuni, who's entire face switched to kindness. Their stern look returned when Marissa returned to her daughter, "I didn't know *anyone* in Northern Rulo was looking for me besides the hunters."

"And me? What about me?" Keyona sharply inquired. "Are there hunters that are gonna come for me now? *Did* any hunters come for me ever? Are you gonna go back with Ipkuni or whatev–"

"I can't go back with Ipkuni, Keyona." Agitation flooded under Marrisa's tone. "I have a family and a life now! I can't uproot all that and return to Rulo! I have a job at the office here, I have a family here, I have a *home* here." She noticed what she just said and switched to Ipkuni, they were clearly stung from the remark. "Ipi, I'm ... I'm ..."

Ipkuni looked away, dejected. Their lashes and eyes filtered a soft plum blue.

Marissa sighed. She placed a hand on Ipkuni's shoulder, "I just can't go back. Not like this. So much time has passed between our worlds. And I have a *daughter*. What if the hunters got her? We can't play dead now, they'll know. She has my scribe and knows *nothing* about Ruloan customs, she'd be caught quickly."

Ipkuni turned back to Marissa. They opened their mouth but simply didn't know what to say. With a little more thought, they agonized, "I looked *so* far and long for you. We don't have to stay in Rulo. Polis has a sanctuary law for different spirit scribes now and–"

"Ipi, Rulo is our *lives*. We're Ruloans, you know Polis folks don't like us," Marrisa retorted. "We'd go from being tracked in our own homeland to unwanted refugees in another. It's just safer for me to stay *here*. With my family and our lives. Yes, the people here are very weird and no one really makes sense half of the time but it's home. It's Keyona's home, especially. No one knows I have a scribe and that's great–"

"You're wasting your potential, Amika! I can't just *leave* you here. You're ... you're my best friend." Ipkuni eyes and lashes shifted to a deeper plum blue, "I learned *so* much from you, you were my mentor. You accepted my fractured spirit scribe and taught me everything I know. Even my own parents couldn't do that. I just ... I just can't *leave* you here, caged and forgetting your ways."

Marissa sighed and rubbed her forehead, "Ipi, Keke's got most of my scribe now. That's why you got her instead of me. And look at her, she can't live in Rulo. She can barely handle being a few miles – a few revoles, Ipi – up the coastline." Keyona winced. "She knows how to build computers and technology, Rulo doesn't have these things."

"She can *learn*, Amika. If she has your spirit scri–"

"What she gonna do if a hunter catches her, huh?" Marissa stressed. "She can't do illusions. She can't fly, never practiced. She would be a sittin–"

"'Never *practiced*'?!" Keyona erupted. "What you mean by '*never practiced*'! I can do this? I can fly?" Her face darted between Ipkuni and Marissa. "I can fly? Momma, why you never teach me how to do this?"

Marissa shot, "Because *airplanes* exist and you don't need to attract attention! These hunters are *nothin'* to play with, Keyona. And here, if it ain't hunters, it's crazy scientists. You are *not* gonna disappear over nothin' as foolish as flyin'!" Marissa was practically booming. She collected herself to resume at a normal volume to Ipkuni.

"Ipi, she's just not *built* for that world. Look, you can visit but I can't come back. Please understand, Ipkuni. You're my best friend and I miss Rulo but there's too much of a time difference. You still look young but look at how much I've aged." The years sagged her skin, wrinkles collected around her eyes. She looked nothing of her younger self from so long ago.

"Even more of a reason to come back to our world, what if I visit and you're an old woman? Or worse, dead?" Ipkuni agonized, the jingle in their voice tightening. "Maybe I should stay here in this world. The hunters still suspect me occasionally, too."

Marissa was awestruck. "Ipi, *no*. This world is much too different from ours. You wouldn't know the first thing of what to do here. No one can read our letters or books, you'd be considered illiterate here. Start floatin' and people will freak out. It just wouldn't work!"

"Then what *do* we do then, Amika? I won't let us part ways. Not after all this, not after all we've been through." Ipkuni was determined to not let Amika slip away again.

Marissa pondered for a bit. Empty of a full plan, she said, "We rest. Keke, check on your father and make sure he is still asleep. Ipkuni and I are gonna talk for a little more. Let me know when you did everything."

✿

Marissa and Ipkuni talked late into the night. Keyona had come back to confirm her father snoozing. His snores were as audacious as always, Keyona didn't have to go far to check. After an hour of facing Ipkuni's poisonous stares and one quick violet flash after she asked a question, Keyona excused herself and headed straight to bed.

Most of her room was down in Delaware, all that remained were some pillows, posters on her walls and a lumpy sleeping bag. It wasn't ideal but she was tuckered out enough to drop off in minutes. Meanwhile, Marissa and Ipkuni chattered on like old times. But Marissa never reminisced for too long, an effective plan needed to be hatched. A way to move forward. Ipkuni's mood soured every time she broached the subject but together, they eventually nailed down something. It wasn't a plan they both loved but it was one that would keep them connected.

They both agreed the plan would go into motion bright and early in the morning. Marissa told Ipkuni to hold tight in the storage den, she wanted to get her husband out the way. On the couch, she found her husband snoring loudly under a woven blanket. Terrance gave little fuss, as he always did when Marissa came to wake him up on the couch. Working at the processing plant, there was rarely a day Terrence could keep his eyes open before nightfall. Husband in bed, Marissa came back down to dress the couch for Ipkuni with extra pillows and the softest blanket she could find. She wanted to mimic a Ruloan bed as much as possible. Nothing was as soft or comfy in this world but she tried her best. When she presented the couch to Ipkuni, Marissa could tell they swallowed their disdain for the odd, non-Ruloan bed. Ipkuni hugged her good night.

"I hope this will work, Ipi," Marissa said.

Ipkuni smiled, their eyes brimmed with a subtle, kind glow in the dark living room. "There's always my idea of coming back home. If this doesn't work out, that is what we'll do. Sleep well, Amika."

Amika gave Ipkuni one last hug and sauntered up the stairs. A small dim orb bled from the wall and followed behind her, lighting the way.

Morning came quickly. Marissa's phone rattled beside her arm. The soft hues of dawn drew long shadows across the cluttered room. The room was full with memories and work, the space over-filled with wedding pictures, trinkets of old memories and strewn about work jumpers. She rose with little issue; Marissa didn't want to oversleep and risk her husband stumbling upon Ipkuni. She caught a few of Ipkuni's cold glares at her daughter, she was certain it would be much worse with her husband. Non-scribed and scribed usually got along together but Ipkuni was a lot less ... forgiving than what she remembered. Then again, she couldn't blame them, being a Hunted herself. Marissa silenced the alarm and slipped out of bed. Terrance didn't stir; he always had been a heavy sleeper in all the thirty plus years she had known him. Back when he was in college, she would always wake him, the two alarm clocks by his pillow never did a thing.

Marissa adjusted her wig. She never took it off unless she was sure the house was empty. Marissa grew accustomed to wearing wigs day in and day out. It was uncomfortable but it was better than doing constant illusion work daily like when she first landed in this world. No one outside of her old world had ever seen her real hair, each strand filled from scalp to end with small, clear silver beads. They used to be a beautiful light plum but the years and stress faded them to silver. Marissa silently thanked the stars when Keyona was born with robust tight springs of curls, taking after Terrence. Instead, Keyona took on her plump cheeks and round chin. And most of her spirit scribe instead of half, something normal among scribe births with unscribed people.

Finished with her wig, she opened her nightstand drawer and pulled out a small bag to refresh her makeup. Marissa used the darkest mascara for her lashes, and contacts for her eyes. They changed color, just like Ipkuni and everyone else in Rulo. She was grateful the contacts covered the changes well. Her brows were dyed, to keep life simple. Every time a new, white hair grew and someone pointed it out, Marissa would joke about old age to pass any suspicion. Years on this planet and she still never knew if she was talking to a crafty hunter. They could pull illusions, too. It was normal for their scribe. Never normal for hers.

Marissa finished her makeup, replaced the bag and left her room. She could tell Ipkuni's presence influenced her; for the second time in a full house, she used a dim orb to light her path down the hall. She floated to the stairs like a swan crossing water. It was more comfortable to be herself, a reassurance that she was still alive after all these years on the run. She hovered her hand over the railing, and her bare feet hardly touched the stairs as she descended them. She saw that Ipkuni was awake.

Hovering before Ipkuni was an information orb. With a navy glow, Ruloan text slid across in glittering gold. Ipkuni sat floating and cross-legged as they read. It had been eons since Marissa saw her native language, she could only piece together fragments of what she saw. Ipkuni was trying to pull information about the world they were in and how it functioned.

"Couldn't sleep?" Marissa asked as she drifted to Ipkuni's side. Her light orb dimmed out of existence.

Ipkuni jumped, they almost tumbled out the air as their lashes and eyes flashed to stark topaz. Clutching their heart, Ipkuni sighed into a breathy laugh. It was like old times again, they always stayed up and Amika would always pop up out of nowhere to see what they were doing. The information orb faded into an illumination orb.

As their lashes and eyes paled back to snow, Ipkuni admitted, "I *couldn't* sleep, though I tried. I just can't believe you're *here*, Amika. And with child. With husband." Ipkuni motioned about, still stupefied by the grand size of the house, "With ... with *everything*. I want you home ... but ... what am I pulling you away from? I feel divided." Their tone bore a deep, solemn jangle.

Marissa placed a hand on Ipkuni's shoulder. She remembered the old times they both spent back in Rulo. How she would watch Ipkuni dart about on the surface of lakes and splash about in rivers, careless and free. How she honed their scribe from a tempest of unpredictable and wild energy to one of strength and capability. She felt proud the day Ipkuni could mimic her abilities. Such a wonder of a student, one she never thought she would live to see reach their fullest potential. Some days, memories of how she met Ipkuni would drift to her out the blue, how they were huddled under a merchant's booth in a battered shawl trying to use their scribe to lift bread and fruit out the baskets of passerby. When she caught Ipkuni doing the same to her, she was enraged until she saw the starving look on their face. Instead of handing Ipkuni over to a nearby hunter, she decided to take them in. And now, there Ipkuni stood before her, dressed in fine cloth, prim and proper.

"Ipi, don't feel bad," Marissa consoled. "I want to go home, too."

Ipkuni's face darted up, their lashes and eyes brightened as a small smile slid onto their face.

"But ... I *can't*." Marissa could never become Amika again. The hunters would just come back in full force, they never stop until death or capture. And with her family? Impossible.

Ipkuni looked away, hurt. They wanted so much to take Amika back home, to make things right for not listening the first time.

Marissa frowned, "I want to, but it just isn't that easy anymore. That's why Keyona should be in my place–"

"She isn't one of us!" Ipkuni protested. Their eyes and lashes slipped into a stormy gray from frustration. "She doesn't *understand* anything! She's more *kulaian* than–"

"'*Kulaian*'?" Amika repeated, aghast. It was an awful term to describe outsiders. "She is my *daughter*, Ipi. Please, never call her that again. She is no more kulaian than I am. She is half Ruloan, yes, but that does *not* make her any part kulaian."

The gray grew shades of lavender as Ipkuni seethed, "From the little time I have spent with her, Amika, she was *nothing* like you. You're brave and capable and willing! She is scatterbrained and aimless! What can I give her?"

Astonished, Amika reminded them in a hushed tone, "How does that make her any different than how you were when I first met you? You were *not* always like this. You were just as aimless, just as–"

"I simply needed a teacher!" Ipkuni strained under their quieted voice, jangling with bass. "I had passion! She has none! She walked us through a forest for*ever*. You would have had a *plan*."

"She was tossed into a world she never knew, with abilities she didn't even know she had until mere hours ago!" Amika hissed. "How d'you *expect* her to behave? She was terrified, Ipi. She's not a planner, she just *does*. That's Keke for you. But that doesn't mean she's not worth bein' around. And she was the bridge that led you back to me." Amika watched Ipkuni's eyes and lashes soften to snow blue at the realization. "Shouldn't that count for somethin'? Anything?"

Ipkuni considered Amika's words. Though they sincerely pegged Keyona the grandest fool to grace Rulo, Amika was right.

Amika placed her hand under the lumination orb, two more divided from the sides to provide more light. The sun was soon to come up, she could see the faint dawning of the morning light. Soon, the work alarm on her husband's phone would rattle and ring.

She beckoned Ipkuni to the red hallway, "C'mon, let's get you hidden before my husband gets confused." She sighed to herself as she helped Ipkuni up from the couch, "One surprise at a time."

As they both floated down the hall together, the orbs trailing behind them, Amika promised, "I'll make you breakfast but be warned: Things are different here. Even the eggs taste different, so don't expect anything too amazing."

"What about dramli bread?" Ipkuni inquired, their voice returned to a normal chime.

"There isn't even dramli *here* in this world, Ipi. I've looked *everywhere*. The closest these people have is something called 'pumpernickel' and it just isn't the same. Not even by a long shot."

❧

The sun shone bright through Keyona's room, a flicker of dappled light across her face stirred her but the blaring arrhythmic wail of her father's phone at the other end of the hall was what woke her up. The wails filled the second floor. This usually woke everyone up ... but him.

By the time Keyona dragged herself out of her room, the alarm stopped. The heavy smell of eggs and homefries hung in the air. Pans sizzled below; breakfast was on the stove.

Keyona missed home cooked meals. Scratching her stomach and fixing her satin scarf, Keyona shuffled barefoot down the cream hall into her parents' room.

Her father, a tired old man with a grizzled face, still laid in bed. His eyes were barely parted. The sun light beamed above his head. By his side sat Marissa, she had his quiet phone in her lap and rocked him from time to time to ensure he wouldn't drift back to sleep. Rarely did Keyona see her father not sleep like the dead.

Propped against the doorway, Keyona smirked, "Dad, you still need Ma to wake you up?"

Terrence looked over. He blinked a couple times. His face brightened at the sight of his daughter and he sat up. The years spent working with heavy machines showed in his joints. Marissa beamed at her daughter and rubbed her husband's back.

"Well, hi there, stranger," Terrance chuckled, sleep nestled deep in his voice. He propped himself to one side and extended his arm, "Why don't you give me a hug?"

Keyona bounded into his arms and snuggled against him. Her father kissed her on the head and asked, "When did you get in?"

Marissa kept her warm smile but a slight pang of anxiety flitted within her.

"Last night," Keyona answered. "Took a late train in for a surprise visit for the weekend."

A quiet sigh escaped from Marissa's lips. Keyona didn't forget her lines or the alibi. In their practice back in the storage room, Keyona screwed up so much, she was sure Ipkuni was mentally preparing a puppet incantation just to cut everything short and return to reminiscing.

Terrance rubbed Keyona's back, "Oh, really? And what a wonderful surprise it is." He turned to Marissa and asked, "Did you know Keyona would be around?"

"I ran into her last night after you went to bed when I was going to the bathroom," Marissa lied. She never liked to fib to her only love but it was revoles better than explaining the truth.

Terrance brimmed a wider smile, he had small teeth and slightly crooked canines. His family was back together again. But he lamented, "Oh, I can't call out today, Keke. And I'mma have to go soon but how long you gonna be here? I don't want you missin' any interviews or nothin'."

A small stake jabbed Keyona's heart, but she smiled through it, "I'll be gone on Monday."

Terrance pecked her on the cheek. "Oh, okay. Don't you go nowhere far, I wanna catch up with you when I get off work, y'hear?"

"Ok, Dad," Keyona nodded. She told her mother, "I'mma

be downstairs before the food gets burnt. See y'all later."

Both of her parents waved as Keyona left. She trumped down the stairs and went into the kitchen to turn all the burners low. Every eye of the stove had something simmering and sizzling: fluffy scrambled eggs, peppered homefries, simmering grits and sizzling sausage patties. What a symphony of smells to entice her but she was eager to see Ipkuni. Keyona ran down the hall, quiet but excited. She yanked opened the storage room door and found herself face to face with a startled Ipkuni, eyes and lashes turned to blackened topaz. They sprang back, clutching their heart.

As Keyona closed the door, Ipkuni wheezed, "Don't *scare* me like that! You came in here like a hunter!"

Keyona flittered a quick apology, a Cheshire smile painted across her face, "Sorry! I just wanna know how to fly an' stuff!" She fizzed with eagerness, she could barely contain her excitement.

Ipkuni felt the opposite, their lashes and eyes turned from black topaz to a stony lavender blue. "Keyona, I can't just *teach* you how to whiz into the sky, that's not how any of this works. You don't even know how to summon your spirit scribe–"

"Then show me *hooow*!" Keyona begged impatiently. She didn't want to spare another second in wait, Keyona wanted to explore all that she had stored deep inside her. Particularly the cooler stuff first.

"Not until your mother arrives, Keyona," Ipkuni reminded, irritated. Their voice jangled with a slow bass chime. "That is what she told you and I shall not move from Amika's word."

Keyona rolled her eyes and blustered a defiant sigh. She stuck out a hand, bemused, "Not even a small trick? Like makin' those light balls you do–"

"Not without *Amika*." Ipkuni lifted from the floor, their eyes shifted to a deep violet.

Keyona's face fell ashen, she started to back away. She tapped against the door, startled by the dead end.

Drawing closer and closer to Keyona, Ipkuni seethed quietly with a tight jingle in their deep voice, "You have *tested* my patience since the *moment* I met you. Listen to me when I say you *must* have Amika with you to practice and that I will *not* have it any other way." With their head knelt over Keyona, they continued, "I am *only* doing this for dear Amika, and you will *remember* this. Do *not* test me further, child. If I could pry that scribe out of your being with my own two hands and put it back in her, I would. Am. I. *Clear*?"

Rattled, Keyona nodded.

Ipkuni lowered to the floor, their eyes and lashes fading back to snow. Their voice became a firm jingle, "Good. Now, go get your mother. She said there would be breakfast? It may be kul-ehh… *different* from what she and I are used to but I am quite famished." They gleamed a plastic smile.

Riveted to the spot, Keyona patted about for the knob. She turned it and slipped out, never breaking eye contact with Ipkuni.

Carefully, Keyona closed the door and hurried down the hall. In the dining room, she found her parents at the breakfast table, everything laid out on large serving plates. Her father had on his worn, navy jumpsuit, zippered to his bearded throat. He was head supervisor but he still had plenty of manual labor to do. The only difference between him and the workers he looked after was more paperwork and heard more nagging from the top. His plate was almost empty, he worked on the last of his eggs. Marissa had a half empty plate, and a full one waited for Keyona.

Terrance beamed at his daughter, "I'm so glad I could see you before I head off to work. Gimme a hug, baby girl."

Keyona wrapped her arms around her father. She was indeed glad to see him, it had been so long since she nestled in his arms – but she also needed comfort after Ipkuni terrified her. Terrance pecked her on the cheek, she pecked back. He smelled of hickory spice, just like since she was a little girl. Her heart soothed.

His plate clean, Terrance broke the embrace and rose

up, "I'll catch you when I get off, okay?" He shuffled his way to the door, a smile etched on his face.

Keyona waved, "Okay, Dad! Have a good day at work!"

"Bye, honey!" Marissa chimed.

Terrance return their wave and left, the door clicked shut.

Marrisa sighed, "Finally outta here." She returned to the kitchen to fix an extra plate. "Keke, go get Ipi and let's eat," Marissa directed as she tapped food onto the plate in small, neat, separated portions.

Keyona's stomach dropped a little. She wanted to say "No way, I'm terrified" but that would have probably delayed the task. Keyona plucked up whatever bravery she was sure she didn't have and returned down the hall.

"Ipkuni!" Keyona called out as she inched down the hall. "Breakfast is ready!"

At the end of the hall, the storage door sprang open and out hovered Ipkuni. The sun caught the glimmer of their neat, braided hair. Like a shot, Ipkuni speared down the hall. Keyona almost unhinged a portrait with her shoulder dodging them.

Ipkuni curved around the corner and landed at the table, spying the food presented for them. Never had they ever seen such fare before. Ruloan food was much more colorful than this paltry mess that graced their plate, perfectly quartered.

Marissa saw Ipkuni's twisted face. "Ipi, I know this ain't Ruloan but at *least* give it a try."

Keyona returned to the breakfast table and picked up her plate to sit close to her mother. They were almost shoulder to shoulder. She tried to hide the troubled waver in her voice as she asked, "Ma, he's never seen this kind of food before?"

"Keke!" Her mother reeled. "Have you been calling them 'sir' or 'mister' this whole time?"

Ipkuni sniffed at their puddle of grits and winced away, chiming lowly, "Sometimes 'ma'am' or 'miss'." They dipped their tongue in the grits. The taste and texture were similar to palemeal back in Rulo but that was considered more of a dinner meal than a breakfast one.

Marissa stared at Keyona, floored.

Keyona didn't understand what she screwed up now. "Wh-what?!" she blustered.

Marissa explained, "Keke, Ipi is neither. Just ... Ipi, I'm so sorry," she apologized to her longtime friend. "Things work a little different in this world and Keke is still young. This is not as well taught here as I would like but Keke," she returned to her daughter, "Keke, just stick to their name for now, okay?"

Still lost, Keyona gave up, "Fine, okay." She changed the subject, a little more confident now that her mother was beside her, "Ma, can y'all show me some stuff now? Ipkuni said that I can't learn nothin' without you around."

Ipkuni took a ginger bite of their sausage. Greasy and very much not like home. "Amika, she needs to learn how to summon her scribe before even trying anything else. We don't even know what it looks like."

Keyona tugged at her mother, excitement washing over her fear, "Ma! What yours look like?"

Marissa gave her daughter an unsure glance. It had been many moons since she saw it herself and since she gave birth to Keyona, she hadn't really checked. She could feel a good bit of it was gone already, she didn't need to see.

Ipkuni urged her also. "Show her, Amika."

Marissa gazed at her empty plate. She looked back at her daughter, "It's been a while, baby. And you have most of it." Marissa turned to Ipkuni, "Ipi, can you show her? It might take me a while to pull mine up."

Ipkuni nodded. They pushed away their plate and presented their hand before their chest. Ipkuni closed their eyes and steadied their breath. A jagged gem blurred into view, it held fades of charcoal black between the breaks of gray. Pockmarks covered the surface, but no other markings. The gem rotated freely and slowly over their palm.

Keyona's jaw dropped.

Marissa explained to Keyona, "That's Ipi's spirit scribe. There's supposed to be markings on it and have a smooth surface but theirs isn't. Not their fault, just how they were born. But back in Rulo–"

"Back in Rulo, I'm an Unwanted," Ipkuni finished, their eyes still closed. The gem faded away and Ipkuni lowered their hand. Opening their eyes, Ipkuni explained, careful with their words, "I'm ... I'm not designated for anything. This ... bothered my parents."

Marissa filled in, "Every spirit scribe is supposed to look a certain way, to determine who you will be in life. Ipi doesn't have what is considered normal, so that made Ipi an Unwanted, which is an underclass in Ruloan society. I trained them because I sensed they could do a little bit of everything."

Ipkuni smiled at the compliment. Their eyes and lashes blushed a light peach.

"I guess I should try, now," said Marissa. She did the same as Ipkuni, she closed her eyes, raised her hand and steadied her breath. It took a couple tries but a small sea blue pebble blurred into view, hovering and rotating. It was smooth, clear and with deep ruby markings covering the center of it, three jagged lines crossed together.

Keyona marveled at the sight. It wavered before her eyes, then disappeared.

Marissa opened her eyes, she felt the scribe disappear. It disappointed her she couldn't hold it as long as she used to. "That's all that's left. The rest is in you, Keke."

"How ... how do I get it?" Keyona asked, anxious and eager.

Ipkuni and Amika exchanged glances. The knowledge was usually considered innate for scribed individuals but as Keyona was only half-scribed and so far removed from any Ruloan customs or culture, it was evident she would have to be taught.

This left her mother a little stumped, "Uhhhh .... You put your hand in front of you, like this." She placed her hand in front of her chest. Keyona copied. "And you close your eyes." Keyona shut her eyes. "Keep your breath steady and think of my scribe," Marissa described softly. "Try to pull it up."

Ipkuni watched intently as Keyona held her hand in front of her chest, eyes closed and with a focused breath. She imagined her mother's small scribe floating before her. Holding to that image tightly, Keyona imagined it again and again. The smoothness of the pebble, the gentle frost inside, the starkness of the marking. Its vibrant color stood out most in her mind.

Soon, she heard her mother gasp and Ipkuni marvel breathless, "How ... this scribe is ... it has Scholar colors in the marking but ... it's so different!"

Keyona opened her eyes slowly. In her palm floated a glittering stone rotating with ease. It had waves of sea blue and gold. A strange, dark red etch sat in the center. It looked like a crossed-out spiral.

Stupefied by the brilliance, Ipkuni jingled, "It shimmers like a million stars. How new! And this mark ... Amika, what does it mean? I have never seen it before."

Never had Amika seen such a scribe or an etch, it was completely new. All etches were Ruloan, it's what the language blossomed from, but this was absolutely new. A new word, a new meaning. In Rulo, the shimmering blue and gold would have already made her an outcast, as was being a half-scribe. But the etch? It would have been deemed un-Ruloan, a false scribe. Keyona would have spent the rest of her lifetime avoiding hunters, just like her mother.

But it didn't have to be that way.

Her mother drew up a kind smile, "This means that she's very special, but it's up to her to define what that special is."

Keyona didn't understand, neither did Ipkuni.

"What?" They both asked, befuddled.

Amika looked at Keyona, her eyes filled with pride and sadness. "I should have never hid this from you. Your scribe is odd but it just means you have undiscovered potential. Just like Ipkuni. Just like me." She unhooked and slid off her wig. Long, braided tendrils of beaded hair fell upon her shoulders. They clattered together as they poured around her neck. She threw her arms around Keyona, tears streaming down her face.

The scribe dropped away from the broken concentration. Keyona had never known what her mother hid from her in plain sight. Keyona's eyes beaded with tears at the realization of how much of herself she truly did not know – but she was determined to make up for lost time.

Amika choked with elation as she held her daughter, "I'm so proud of you. Whatever you'll become, it will be magnificent."

Other works

Null(Void)

About the Author

MultiMind lives in Baltimore, Maryland. She tries to find time for her countless hobbies, from 3D printing to bookbinding to virtual reality. And her vociferous cat. She writes books that are fairly Black, quite queer, and very much embedded in the world of Sci-Fi, Fantasy & Horror.